Cornelius

Cornelius

a fable by Leo Lionni

Alfred A. Knopf
New York

When the eggs hatched,
the little crocodiles crawled out
onto the riverbeach.
But Cornelius walked out *upright*.

As he grew taller and stronger,
he rarely came down on all fours.
He saw things no other
crocodile had ever seen before.
"I can see far beyond the bushes!"
he said.
But the others said,
"What's so good about that?"

"I can see the fish from above!" Cornelius said.
"So what?" said the others, annoyed.

And so one day, Cornelius angrily decided to walk away.

It was not long before he met a monkey.
"I can walk upright!" Cornelius said proudly.
"And I can see things far away!"

"I can stand on my head," said the monkey.

"And hang from my tail."
Cornelius was amazed. "Could I learn to do that?" he asked.

"Of course," replied the monkey. "All you need is a lot of hard work and a little help."

Cornelius worked hard
at learning the monkey's tricks,
and the monkey seemed happy
to help him.

When he had finally learned to stand on his head
and hang from his tail,
Cornelius walked proudly back to the riverbeach.

"Look!" he said. "I can stand on my head."
"So what!" was all the others said.

"And I can hang from my tail!"
said Cornelius.
But the others
just frowned and repeated,
"So what!"

There the others were, falling all over themselves
trying to stand on their heads and hang from their tails!
Cornelius smiled. Life on the riverbeach
would never be the same again.

THIS IS A BORZOI BOOK PUBLISHED BY ALFRED A. KNOPF

Copyright © 1983 by Leo Lionni

All rights reserved. Published in the United States by Alfred A. Knopf, an imprint of Random House Children's Books,
a division of Penguin Random House LLC, New York. Originally published in hardcover by Pantheon Books, New York, in 1983.

Knopf, Borzoi Books, and the colophon are registered trademarks of Penguin Random House LLC.

Visit us on the Web! randomhousekids.com

Kohls.com/Kids

Educators and librarians, for a variety of teaching tools, visit us at RHTeachersLibrarians.com

This special edition was printed for Kohl's Department Stores, Inc. (for distribution on behalf of Kohl's Cares, LLC,
its wholly owned subsidiary), by Random House Children's Books, a division of Penguin Random House LLC, New York.

Kohl's
1415115-00
123387
08/15 – 10/15

ISBN 978-0-375-97501-1

MANUFACTURED IN CHINA
10 9 8 7 6 5 4 3 2 1